The Secret Friend

by Marcia Vaughan
Illustrated by John Sandford

HOUGHTON MIFFLIN

Boston · Atlanta · Dallas · Geneva, Illinois · Palo Alto · Princeton

One day Squirrel found something on his tree.

"A letter! A letter! And it's for me!"

To Squirrel

2

Dear Squirrel,
I like you!
xxxooo
Your Secret Friend
(Can you guess who?)

3

"Fox," said Squirrel,
"Is this letter from you?"
"No," said Fox.
"I got one, too."

4

Dear Fox,
   I like you!
xxxooo
   Your Secret Friend
   (Can you guess who?)

5

"Bear," said Fox,
"Are these letters from you?"
"No," said Bear.
"I got one, too."

To Bear

"Moose," said Bear,
"Are these letters from you?"
"No," said Moose.
"I got one, too."

Dear Moose,
  I like you!
xxx ooo
    Your Secret Friend
    (Can you guess who?)

"Owl," said Moose,
"Are these letters from you?"
"No," said Owl.
"I got one, too."

11

The animals thought,
"Who can it be?"

"Surprise!" cried Snake.
"Your secret friend is me!"

13

The very next day
Snake found something on his tree.

14

"A letter! A letter! And it's for me!"

Dear Snake,
we like you, too!
xxxooo
Your five new friends
(Can you guess who?)

16